A cool little book of big ideas,
Jawbreakers is a wonderful celebration
of flash fiction.
Nik Perring

This is, quite simply, one of the best
collections of stories I've seen in a very long
time. Covering every conceivable emotion,
genre and style, the stories have only this in
common: they are extremely well written
and a delight to read.
Lorraine Mace— *Flash 500*

Beautiful. Overwhelmingly brief.
Wonderful. Epically quick.
Perfect. Massively short.
In the time it takes to drink a glass of water,
they balance a world on your tongue.
Matt Shoard—*Fleeting Magazine*

Tight, brief, tense and precise,
these stories throw us in-and-out of the
human condition in deep and surprising
ways. What better than a finger-on-the-pulse
anthology of flash to seduce the modern
reader? Read and be thrilled.
Nuala Ní Chonchúir

Jawbreakers is a total treat.
This exhilarating collection
of flash fiction, will leave you breathless
and gasping for more...
Frances Everitt—*Bridport Prize*

If, like me, you end up reading this
anthology in one sitting, ... hold on to your
hat! *Jawbreakers* is packed with stories that
will take you to places you
never knew existed.
Vic Errington— *Flash Fiction World*

Jawbreakers

A collection of flash-fictions

Edited by
Calum Kerr and Valerie O'Riordan

A National Flash-Fiction Day and Completely Novel Publication
Supported using public funding by Arts Council England

First Published 2012 by National Flash-Fiction Day
in association with CompletelyNovel.com
Supported using public funding by Arts Council England

National Flash-Fiction Day
18 Caxton Avenue
Bitterne
Southampton
SO19 5LJ
www.nationalflashfictionday.co.uk

Cover image ©2012 Andy Broadey
(http://www.bankley.org.uk/Artist-Andy-Broadey)
Cover design by Andy Broadey and Calum Kerr.
Typeset by Calum Kerr.

A CIP Catalogue record for this book
is available from the British Library

ISBN 978-1-84914-285-4

For Flash-Fictioneers everywhere!

Contents

Micro-fiction Competition Winners:

The Worst Head in the World

Foreword

Welcome to *Jawbreakers*, an anthology of flash-fictions from fifty-eight diverse and talented writers. Here you will find stories encompassing nearly every imaginable genre, style, perspective and emotion, each one delivering the goods in five-hundred words or fewer.

But what *exactly*, you may be asking, are these things called 'flash-fictions'?

Well, we're talking short, short stories. Exact definitions vary; pedants will shake their fountain pens and argue over word-counts—the sub-one-thousand-word brigade clashes swords at dawn with the one-hundred-word army—but there's no real consensus. Short-shorts, micro-fictions, flash-fictions or Hemingway's alleged trump-card, the six-word story ('For sale: baby shoes, never worn.'): what unites all these factions is brevity. These are tiny, concise tales that condense, like our titular jawbreakers, an enormity of flavour and energy into a very dense space. And it's in this condensation that the secret of flash-fiction lies.

These are stories that, in a mere couple of paragraphs, match the power and impact of considerably longer works. Like short stories and novels, flash-fictions want to move you, to shake and entertain you, to lift you, to make you laugh and cry and think. Like poems, they want to conjure up the entirety of a world in half a page and make that world linger long beyond the time it took for you to read the story. Whilst we believe that writing of any length ought to be considered and precise, the reduced word-count of flash-fiction puts that precision under a critical microscope: with no leeway for the reader to skim or to lose concentration; every word simply must count. And that's undoubtedly the case with each story in this collection. The writers here have crafted perfect, miniature worlds for every page; their language, their characters and their startling imaginations bear the same weight as any thousand-page doorstopper.

This collection has been produced as part of the UK's first National Flash-Fiction Day (16th May 2012) and features some of the very best writers working in flash-fiction. Here you will find flashes by Ian Rankin, Jenn Ashworth, Tania Hershman, Vanessa Gebbie, David Gaffney, Jonathan Pinnock, Valerie O'Riordan, Calum Kerr and more—including a special micro-fiction from Ali Smith. We've also included the winners and runners-up of a micro-fiction competition we ran back in early 2012, so you'll find, at the end of the book, ten stories of one-hundred words or fewer—each one a tiny gem.

National Flash-Fiction Day was conceived by Calum as a way to bring together the country's flash-fiction writing community, to celebrate this form of story and bring it to the attention of the wider public. He felt this was necessary because, while short, short stories have been around as long as literature, it has only really been in the last twenty years that they have started to take off as something separate. He felt that flash-fiction was ready for its close-up—and as you can see from the book in your hands, many people agreed.

We hope you enjoy *Jawbreakers*. It has been a fantastically enjoyable experience to put it together, and we're extremely proud of the collection, believing it represents some of the very finest flash-fiction ever brought together in a single volume.

Calum Kerr
Valerie O'Riordan
April 2012

Quick

Ali Smith

Once upon a time
               gentlemen please.

Jawbreakers

Jen Campbell

I only used t'steal from the collection bowl so me and Toni could buy gobstoppers at the Grassmarket. And, anyway, it wasn't really stealin'. Me mam put a quid in, and the stoppers were half that. Sometimes, dad says, people at church can be greedy as owt, so I don't feel too bad. We were greedy an' all.

We'd buy the big kind, the ones that would near choke ya if you didn't suck 'em right. We'd skip maths class and sneak over to the cliff tops. Suck 'em as the wind blew in our faces, throwin' stones at the seagulls. When the bell rang we'd shove the stoppers back in their paper bags, all sticky in our pockets. If they got ruined, we'd lob them at kids on the bus home.

"They're like the world, innit?" Toni said, spit dripping off her chin, her cheeks filled out like rock hard balloons.

"Aye," I said, nodding. Balancing the whole world on my tongue.

Peekaboo

Dan Powell

The Health Visitor knocks the door. The Health Visitor knocks the door and my heart jack rabbits. The Health Visitor knocks the door and I can't find my daughter.

'I was knocking,' the woman says when I finally answer. She waves a clipboard ahead of her as she enters. 'Did you not hear?'

My eyes dart up the stairs, along the hall, back out the still open door. Somewhere I hear Molly giggle.

'So,' says the Health Visitor. She introduces herself though I know her name from the letter that arrived last week. She is all efficiency with her well cut skirt, her bag of tricks designed to test a child's development, the click of her platinum plated pen like a starting pistol. 'Where is,' she consults her paperwork, 'Where is Molly?'

When toddlers put their hands over their eyes they think that *you* can't see *them*.

'Moll-Moll,' my daughter says in a sing-song voice that sounds like she is in the room. I think she is definitely in the room.

When toddlers put their hands over their eyes the normal thing is they *think* that you can't see them.

'Molly.' I try my best Mommy tone in the hope she will put her hands down but she doesn't. She just giggles again.

The Health Visitor looks around the room, a perplexed grimace filling her face. She checks her watch.

'I take it Molly is here?'

Molly laughs now.

'Is that coming from the baby monitor?' The Health Visitor looks down at her papers, selects one, fixes it to the top of her clipboard. 'Now, Molly is eighteen months, just over?' I nod and hand her my daughter's red book. She flicks through the pages to the weight development graph. 'All good there,' she says and looks at me. 'Could you please fetch Molly? I have another child at eleven.'

And right then Molly pulls her hands away and blinks back into view. Where just seconds before there was empty space, my daughter appears on the coffee table wearing just a nappy, plump with wee.

Molly giggles again. I stare at the Health Visitor who is staring at Molly. The woman shakes her head for a moment as if she is in a cartoon and just been hit on the head with a hammer. I almost see birds swirling round her head as she slumps back on the sofa in a dead faint.

I take the platinum plated pen from her limp fingers and do my best to fill in the forms in something like the woman's handwriting.

*

'You drifted off there, for a moment,' I say to the Health Visitor when she comes round.

'No, everything seems normal, you said so yourself, see,' I say and point to the filled forms.

'Please, don't apologise,' I say as I see her out.

I close the door, and turn just in time to see Molly, stood in the hall, put her hands to her eyes.

Flight

Vanessa Gebbie

There was a female sealion learned to fly just the once, on the night of a storm, when waves were higher than they'd ever been, the walls were breached and rocks were strewn with things from the sea, living and dead and somewhere between. She flew to the cattle field behind the strand and fell to earth by the standing stones where a heifer, at her first attempt, had given up trying to give early birth, lain down and died - but her bull calf had come, after all that.

The next day, when the storm had blown itself out, the cowman came down to check that all was well, and found the new calf asleep against the body of the sealion - the rich milk on his muzzle smelling strangely of salt, and fish, and sea.

Repetition

Amy Mackelden

Jack says by heart's a push and, if anything, you learn in spite of your heart, which spins like a confused compass, not entirely sure where north is, or if north is even what you'd want if you found it. It's just a turn of phrase, I say. Just a way of saying confirmation's important, that it can be, that some people learn by repeating. Jack raises an eyebrow, creates a crease, threatens skin folds and dimples, but it's a pre-earthquake tremor.

Jack says we look at life differently. I ask him how that is, expecting another of his excuses about why we'll never work, even though eight months to me is past probation, at the end of gestation, getting ready for hatching, or moving in.

You think, Jack says, that love is learning telephone numbers, reciting play lines, like saying Kr on the table is Krypton, like knowing that is knowing everything. But this isn't maths, it's not multiplication – there's no formula to it. And Jack says, if you try to do it over, repeat what you've heard on TV, I'll call you parrot, call you out for it, for cramming, say that you're mugging me, because there's nothing concrete in just repeating what you've heard elsewhere.

And in this way, Jack's more romantic than Matt Damon.

Rivals

Laura Wilkinson

The race is about to begin; gun aimed at the pewter sky. But the girls' eyes are fixed ahead, looking down the white line of the track. Blue sashes quiver against the pounding of young hearts. Team Saint Andrew is a winner.

An explosion, a puff of smoke, and they are off, galloping down the course, wind in their ears, blooms on their cheeks. Ruth is small and light; Mandy is solid, tall for her age. They make a good piggy-back team. There is nothing ahead but the finishing tape. The screaming crowd fades to a blur on the edges of vision. They canter on.

But Mandy's legs grow tired: there's heaviness in her thighs, despite the desire for victory. 'Practise, practise, we have to practise,' Ruth had said. Mandy hears the panting of another rider approaching. A sharp pain. A kick against her buttocks. The finishing line is within reach. They can win.

Ruth's arms tighten round Mandy's throat. Mandy dips her head and pushes her chest forward. Everything closes in. She can hear Ruth's bark above the roar of the crowd, 'Giddy up, Horsey, giddy up!' Before Mandy falls she sees the yellow glint of the Saint David girls' sashes.

When she opens her eyes, Ruth is shrieking. Hysterical. 'You know what happens to old racehorses, don't you? Sent to the knacker's yard. Turned into dog food. Stinky, squishy, lumpy old dog food.' Ruth tears off her sash; throws it to the ground. Mandy crawls to where it lies, and as she picks it up she catches the pin of Ruth's sack race winner's ribbon. A bead of blood gleams at her. She watches Ruth crossing the field, pigtails flouncing. Mandy stands, throws the ribbon down, and stamps on it again and again, until it is buried in the muddy earth.

Bonding

David Gaffney

As soon as the wives were out of earshot Gareth leaned over to Howard and said in a conspiratorial tone, 'Hey, Howard, we have something in common.'

Howard laughed, awkwardly. He'd invited Gareth out because he'd been advised that if he became more socially engaged with his subordinates they would see him as a human being and not just a blob on an organogram.

'Oh yes?'

'Yes.' Gareth leaned forward again and said in a hissy high voice he thought no one could hear, 'We both have fat wives.'

He grinned. 'Eh? Eh? They are both very fat, and we are both slim. It's something we should talk about. A bond.'

Over Gareth's shoulder Howard spotted the wives returning from the toilets and he noticed Belinda smiling at a waiter. Her face was so beautiful and vibrant it broke his heart sometimes what people thought, what people said.

Arabesque

Brindley Hallam Dennis

This guy gets to the Pearly Gates. It's Saint Peter's shift. What? You think that dood skives off just 'cos he's gotta famous name? So St. Peter gets that big ole ledger out an starts flippin' through the pages. He says, what the hell a you dooin' heeya? The guy says ain't I supposed ta be heeya? I jus' come where they sent me. He says, doan tell me I's down fer the other place.

St. Peter says, a course ya ain't down fer the other place. He says, ya done OK. He says, but we warn't expectin' ya jus' yet. He says, what the hell's bin happenin' down there? The guy says, doan ask me, I wus jus' walkin' outta this bar, an' wham, this guy done fills me full a lead.

St. Peter says, no way. He says, we got the cops on that wan. He says, they wus gonna blow the guy away. The guy says, hey, the cops wus there. They done nuthin'. He says, youse gonna get a whole lot more like me. He says, that wus closin' time. He says, I wus leadin' the charge out onta the street.

St. Peter says, sheesh. What the hell them cops thinkin' uv? The guy says, they wus thinkin' a the perpetrator's civil liberties. He says, the guy mighta bin carryin' a table leg for all they noo. He says, he'd got that shooter wrapped up in a plastic bag. St. Peter says, well whooda thought a it?

So the guy says, well, are yas gonna let me in, an' St. Peter says, sure, we got lotsa space up here. He says, but this sure is gonna screw things up for a generation or two. He says, we ain't gonna get this mess sorted out till'n' we get that big ole war off n' started in yo gran'baby's time.

Ed!

Rupan Malakin

Ed works in an office where everyone knows his face, but, he is sure, nobody knows his personality! He is certain his oddities, such as sharing a bed with an army of giant stuffed ants or his nightly snack of cold fish fingers dipped in strawberry yoghurt, would cause his colleagues to do that cocked-head, confused smile thing. In fact, if they could overhear his thoughts right now they may even do the wide-eyed, slow step back common to actors in slapstick comedy.

Ed is thinking: *I'm sick of the 'holding the door open for people' politics in the office.*

He hates the delay if the door is held open too far in advance, which makes people do this gimpy little trot to get there in time, as if he'll let go and leave the door to slam in their face. The worst is when he does the trot, kind of sideways, elbows jutting out, like a line-dancing chicken. And then - *then* - when you get to the door, some people do this swivelling bow as you walk through, like they're some kind of butler. And, to his dismay, Ed has found *himself* doing the bow!

Well, no more.

He is no one's butler.

If it is the last thing I do, thinks Ed, I resolve never again to partake in the office door fiasco. And with that, he marches towards the kitchen to make a coffee, overjoyed to be finally free from such a ridiculous social ordeal.

The kitchen door swings open. Coming out is Sonya from accounts. Ed has always enjoyed a fine relationship with Sonya from accounts, fine meaning he likes how she signs her emails to him with a little smiley face.

Wait. What's this? Why is she holding the door? He's still thirty paces away!

If he ignores her, she'll think him arrogant and never again sign an email with that little smiley face.

If he does the gimpy little trot then he will have recanted on his resolution, which he is loathe to consider.

Ed walks slower, taking shorter steps.

Sonya's smile falters.

It comes to Ed in a flash. He digs his fingers into his ribs, winces, and staggers to the nearest chair. Frowning, he breathes in and out, then shakes his head, glancing up, preparing to smile and say *what the hell was that,* but Sonya is running to him, shouting, "Someone call an ambulance!"

Then Ed is surrounded. Gary from marketing forces him to the floor as Debbie from HR removes his tie, her long blond hair smothering his face. When Ed tries to stand, Gary pushes him down. Medics rush in, roll him onto a stretcher, attach an oxygen mask.

"Grab the door!" cries someone. Gary goes to hold it open.

The medics lift the stretcher. They start to stroll.

Ed looks at them in disbelief – why aren't they hurrying? Can't they see Gary's holding open the door!

Stopwatching

Tania Hershman

I'm tailor-made for timings, she not so much, and so she stands and does the slowness, the almost-creeping still things, and I do the rushings-around, the speedings and flashings-past. It keeps me up and up, I don't tire, I have the limbs and eyes for tracking, even tachyons, no matter speeds of light, of heat, of black, of white or pink or yellow or life or death. I'm thinking beyond death and space and planets, while she, nearly non-breathing, takes care of stasis.

She comes to me, slowly, slowly, once, and tells me, slowly, slowly, all her cares, how her anxiety is more intense than ever, and I glance at her in between my timings, take her in part by part, not understanding what this means, as limes and roses blow between us. I want to question but I don't know the glass of her language, fear my words will burn her with acceleration, so I say nothing and she slinks away.

But as I stopwatch, as I record the darts and dashings, I can't help but notice her gone-ness, where is she now, where does she stand in the trapezoid of toasts and raisings of glasses and smashings of our existence? I slip and trip around to find her but she escapes me, and when Night unhoods I wonder if I might unspeed myself, develocitize. I self-brake and self-brake and when I am at such tardies that I have never tried, there she is.

At these scales and sizes she almost rushes me, she almost swamps me and she's limes and roses blowing and she's all of time and not of time and when she reaches up to me and I reach up to her, there in a moment, minute, parsec, light second, we are still: frozen but not cold, frozen but not dead or dying, frozen there together, smiling.

Favourite

Nathan Good

Your favourite story starts with a young girl.

She is young but not too young. She is old enough that you can see yourself in her. You love to project yourself into stories, especially stories like this.

So it starts with a ten year old girl. She has blonde hair and blue eyes. She has blonde hair and blue eyes because whilst you like to project yourself into stories you do not like the process to be easy. So she doesn't have short black hair and emerald eyes. Her name is not Christine. Your favourite story will be subtle, there will be layers. Her name is Kristy.

Kristy shelters from a light afternoon drizzle beneath the cup of a giant mushroom. The rain turns to small rivulets as it breaks on the forest canopy. By the time it reaches her it has collected the scent of pine. It pools at her feet so she pulls her feet away. She is wearing her best shoes.

Kristy is not going to be safe for long because you are a traditionalist. You like stories that have a clear beginning, middle and end. You require a simple arc of conflict and resolution. So whilst you are enjoying the soft images of a little girl seated on the mossy floor of a forest, you are also starting to feel a little restless. It can not stay so simple, you think, and you enjoy thinking it.

So here is a boy. He is older. He is twenty-seven. And Kristy, she is twenty-seven too. I was wrong before, you like projecting more than I first assumed. They are both twenty-seven and they meet in the pine forest after the rain has stopped. Since the start of the story Kristy has been holding a picnic basket. I just didn't mention it until now. She opens it up and they look inside. The boy has ginger hair, but his name is not Nathan. It is Nate. Nate is looking in the picnic basket and Kristy is looking at Nate.

She has a way of turning her head like an inquisitive bird when she is looking at him. She probably thinks he doesn't notice, but he does.

This story is not going the way I thought it would. I got confused at the end of paragraph two. I can't separate her 'best shoes' from your worn and tired converse flats. I can't have Nate looking into that picnic basket without putting myself right back in the middle of Hyde Park and looking inside that carrier bag.

Kristy looks at Nate and she says, "I don't think this is working."

Nate just sits there. He doesn't even protest. "You don't know anything about me," Kristy says. Then, sick of the giant mushrooms and the smell of pine, she grabs the picnic basket and walks away.

Nate is alone in the forest. "I do know about you," he thinks. And to prove it, he tries to imagine your favourite story.

Inked

Rin Simpson

Alice hoped no one could see the sweat on her forehead. It was too bright in here under the yellow white neon lights, with the sound of Xfm filling the chemical-scented air so there didn't seem to be any room left for oxygen. On the wall a poster of a semi-naked woman, tattooed from neck to navel, raised a pierced eyebrow in what was either amusement or disdain. Either way felt like a challenge. Alice glanced down at the smooth, bare flesh that would soon be covered in black, tribal etchings. It looked so vulnerable, so innocent, so likely to bleed at the slightest touch of a needle. But she knew she mustn't think like that. It was a case of now or never. Taking a deep breath, Alice summoned what she hoped was a confident smile, and looked at her first customer. "Right," she said. "Are we all set?"

Dinghy

Sarah Hilary

In our dinghy, I've packed food for three days and bottled water. If nothing else, the bottles should float.

The spring tide is due, our first in over a year. You should see the sea flexing its muscle, lips smacking the rocks.

It took our shed last week. Now I'll never know what you got up to in there that was so important.

In our dinghy, I've packed food for three days, bottled water and a tarpaulin. I've an idea I can make a sail, if I catch the wind. One of my 'madcap schemes' maybe, but you were the one who wanted this house, teetering at the brink of the world.

'Time to put down roots,' you said, as if I was in danger of dancing away.

In our dinghy, I've packed food for three days, bottled water, a tarpaulin and the cat.

Sorry, because I know you loved the cat, always more than I did. But I can't imagine leaving him here. If this was an inflatable dinghy, I'd think twice about his claws, but it's wood and aluminum, and gawd only knows if it'll float.

In our dinghy, I've packed food for three days, bottled water, a tarpaulin, the cat and your favourite jumper. The cat's taken charge of the jumper, very cosy.

Half the ceiling's down in the back room. We lost nine pantiles from the roof yesterday. You should've heard them swooping like gulls, screeching on the rocks.

Oh, it's all started kicking off, since you went.

I look out to sea twice a day, morning and evening, trying to spy the shed bobbing about. But I guess you went down.

Either that or you're in France already.

M'aidez. M'aidez.

There's a halo round the moon, and another round the sun.

That's rain on the way.

In my dinghy I've packed food for three days, bottled water, a tarpaulin, the cat, your favourite jumper and a compass. That last one's a bit daft, I know. We'll go wherever the tide takes us, maybe straight down.

It's unpicking the house brick by brick. Sucking up the stone and soil of the cliff where we crouched, blind above banks of mist.

If I had any sense, I'd make a run for it, but I've found I can't leave after all, as rooted here as you wanted me to be.

So I'm sleeping in what's left of our home, in the dinghy. With the cat.

I expect we'll be seeing you soon.

Instructions

Sara Crowley

Wash your hands for as long as it takes to sing happy birthday. Dry them counting to ten elephants. Place the yellow, green and red chopping boards on the kitchen top. Fetch vegetables and chicken from the fridge. Worry about cross contamination. Place the chicken on the red board. Prepare veg on the green board - scrape, peel, wash, slice, chop, rinse. Wash your hands for as long as it takes to sing, "Supercalifragilisticexpialidocious!" Smile. Boil water. Select the cook's knife. Ignore the images that flit through your mind of hara-kiri. Dig into chicken flesh. Recoil from tendonsinewmuscle. Wash your hands for as long as it takes to say, "Chick chick chick chick chicken, lay a little egg for me." Scrape the chicken into the bin. Look out of the window. Lawn, flowers, car, neighbour. Wonder how it would feel if you punched a hole through the glass. Hear the front door open. Smile at your daughter.

"Hey lovely, how was your day?"

Pretend you always planned to make a veggie pasta for supper. Grate parmesan onto the yellow board. Listen as your daughter moans about her teacher. Wash your hands to the fastest count of sixteen your mind can conjure. Clear the lunch box debris.

"Twenty minutes until dinner. Go do your homework."

Put the radio on. Jab at the buttons until you hear a song you know and like. Hum. Remember how the guy in the newsagent's winked at you. Daydream a scenario where he declares his uncontrollable desire. Laugh dryly at yourself. Wash your hands for as long as the weather flash on Radio 2 takes. Add the pasta to the largest pan and shake salt into it.

Look at the salt sprinkled on the floor in dismay. Throw some over your left shoulder, then over your right too because you can't remember where the devil sits. Set the timer for twelve minutes.

When you serve the steaming bowls of pasta, smile.

Hammer

Jenn Ashworth

This morning I caught myself picturing the lot of us as leaf-cutter ants. A string of boys swarming down a maze of ginnels carrying treasure to stuff a muddy hollow between an elder and a lilac tree. We had plans to light fires, store contraband, build a look out post – a crow's nest in the branches. Some of us brought plastic milk crates; filched from round the back of the paper shop. Others could only find flattened cardboard boxes, or splintery planks pried from allotment fences. The place stank of cat piss and some mornings we found used condoms in there, but despite its ugliness the den – part burrow, part tree-house – was ours and we built it, rebuilt it, and loved it.

Of course none of us told our parents, but the Hammer Man knew.

I suppose you'd call him a collector and maybe every town has one but he was exotic to us: a grown-up whose treasures were similar to our own. He pushed a bent trolley filled with broken bricks, bundles of knotted carrier bags and the rusting skeletons of bikes and prams. He nicked other people's wheelie bins and hoarded them in his yard.

I don't remember who gave him his name. Not me, I am sure. It must have been because of the tools he brought for us. Screwdrivers with their heads worn smooth. Balls of fraying string and rolls of electrical tape. Old bits of wood and the hammer. We used them all, and sometimes he'd come into the den and help us – his rough hands sure and gentle around ours, guiding the nails in straight, showing how to straighten a bent post or use a rope to make a ladder. He didn't speak, but wheezed and smiled when we did right, rattled his belt buckle and flapped his arms like a dirty bird.

No-one remembers whose dad it was. The day it happened, it was getting dark and we were starting to feel our sunburn. We were inside the den, or hanging off branches, or chipping bark off sticks with stolen penknives and pretending to make kindling. Hammer Man was there, sitting with his back against the trunk of the elder with his hands in his lap rolling one of his nasty cigarettes between his brown fingers. We admired his fingernails: no-one made *him* have baths on Sundays, suffer haircuts, throw away trousers too worn to be worth patching. Who knows what the dad who came to fetch us saw? What that lolling, after a hard days' work, might have looked like?

I ran home.

All I know is this: They broke off his back door, scattered his treasures along the ginnel and kicked in his kitchen window to get at him. When we saw him a few days later, pulling his carrier bag-stuffed trolley behind him, black bruises had bloomed over his face like flowers and he crossed the road to avoid us, as if we were the dirty ones.

Fiver

Bob Jacobs

My wife turned into a five pound note. She was quieter than usual when she slipped into bed that evening, took a few moments longer over her silent prayers. I didn't ask. She liked her space. In the morning the five pound note lay beside me wearing her pyjamas. I was shocked and disappointed. Shocked that after thirty years of marriage Gloria could do something like that without talking to me about it first. Disappointed because what can you buy with five pounds these days?

To begin with Ben and Belinda refused to believe their mother was gone. They cried. Then they became aggressive and demanded equal shares of the five pounds. Of course that was out of the question, you can't split five pounds equally three ways, and they stopped coming round.

I carried the note in my wallet for weeks, wondering what to spend it on. Sometimes I'd get home and gently unfold it, stroke my fingers across the tired looking paper, apologetic almost, like it had been touched by too many hands.

In the end I bought a goldfish. I've named it Gloria. All day long it circles the bowl, mouth opening and closing as if it's trying to tell me something.

Fieldwork

Ian Rankin

'A good agricultural smell,' Rebus muttered. It was an August evening, the sun sinking. The field had been ploughed, but there was no sign of manure. Edinburgh's pathologist, Professor Gates, was crouching over the body of local farmer Dennis Maclay. Rebus peered over his colleague's shoulder.

'Head's been smashed,' he stated.

'Not to mention the urine – whole body's drenched in it.'

Which explained the smell. Rebus looked around. 'Animals?' he guessed.

'Human.' Gates stood up. 'I've seen some things in my time...'

Rebus lit a cigarette. 'How long since it happened?'

'I'd say a good twelve hours.'

'Was he dead when...?'

'He'd have put up a fight, otherwise!'

Rebus could see crows circling the trees at the edge of the field. It was so peaceful out here, six miles west of the city, the motorway a distant drone. Suddenly there was a roar directly overhead: the outline of a passenger jet, making its approach to the airport.

'Professor,' Rebus said quietly. 'You know those stories? Blocks of ice falling from aircraft, jettisoned from the toilets...?' Now Gates raised his eyes, following the plane's progress. 'Hot day like this, how long would it take for something like that to thaw...?'

This story was taken from *Ox-Tales: Earth* (London: GreenProfile, 2009) and *Flash: The International Short-Short Story Magazine*, Volume 4, Number 1, April 2011; reprinted by permission of the author.

Love

Benjamin Judge

Mary Mullane was the first person I met at university.

I had driven for hours. I parked the car in front of the halls and went looking for the Accommodation office. I couldn't find it. I walked back toward my car and I noticed her, standing at the window of a shared kitchen, sprinkling dust into an empty fish tank. Her fingers were long and pale. Her eyes were grey. She wore a yellow handkerchief tied in a loop around her hair, like a 1950s housewife.

We sat next to each other in lectures. We wrote each other little notes. We had nothing in common. We bought two fish for the tank and pretended we didn't see them as a metaphor for our relationship when one of them began to eat the other. We tried to separate them with a piece of plastic. We bought another tank. We split up during the Christmas break.

Pink

Mark Sheerin

There were three of them looking in through the window. In the room there was only one. Syd Barrett, the lost genius of English pop, lay in bed with a blanket pulled over his face. Only the mess of long wavy hair could be seen, confounding rumours of a shaved head. This man was very much asleep, mind you. There would be no conversation.

"There he is," said Ben.

Denny stared at the figure and wished that he could take hold of something, an autograph, a box set or maybe just the memory of an intimate live performance. But the other friend of Ben, a loudmouth called Austin, had already lost interest. He rolled a fag. He was singing quietly and not one of Syd's compositions.

It was a small room with a dirty sink backing onto the hospital grounds, exposed to the glare of passersby. But Syd belonged to a closed off ward, so they couldn't very well visit him as they might a friend. Instead Ben came here to watch the pop star sleep. He often brought guests, such as Austin and Denny.

"His name's not Syd anymore," his glasses sparkled with the news. "His name's Martin Snodge, and he doesn't do much, except cook from time to time."

Denny soaked up this information and gazed at the side of the bed where he'd seen an electric guitar.

"Does he play that thing?"

Ben looked at him as if he was mad.

"I told you," he said quietly. "He does nothing these days."

Along with the guitar there was a record player and a collection of LPs. On top was Aladdin Sane by David Bowie, who was known to have a mad brother. The album reflects his fear of mental illness. You could hear it as "a lad insane," which was how all of them felt. Now he wished he had brought along a camera.

Outside the window the three patients waited for nothing. A hundred cigarette butts on the paving stones pointed the way to excess. Denny picked one up and put it in his pocket. Fancy meeting Syd Barrett, he thought, as a gun boomed in the nearby fields to scare off crows. I'll tell all my friends I met him at a party.

Minutes

Nigel McLoughlin

I see. So you're sure the requirements have all been met?

Yes. It's quite clear: the minutes were received and noted, as you can see from Minute EFC12.03.17B – here, I'll read it to you:
"It was noted that the minute regarding improvements required to be demonstrated in the demographic reports going forward was received at the Demographic Planning and Development Committee and the minute noted in the minutes of that committee (per minute DPD12.02.14C) that the relevant minute from the EFC was received and duly noted, and would be actioned in due course. It was noted in response to a query that this minute will now be forwarded back to the relevant DPD for recording in their minutes with reference to the fact that it has been noted as actioned." So you see it's all in hand.

And what is the action to be taken?

Ah, well, that will be decided by the proper sub-committee of the DPD, depending on whether it relates to departmental recruitment and retention, demographic research, demographic development, demographic refreshment, demographic outreach and consultancy, demographic training enhancement programmes, demographic resource development or employability opportunity enhancement programmes.

Oh, O.K. and which of those deals with the improvements required in the report?

Well, generally, the report is received by all of them, and

because of that the minute related to the report would also be received by all of them, and depending on the particular improvement required, the sub-committee responsible would act by raising the issue in the minutes suggesting action be taken and forward the minute of the decision to action to the DPD for ratification.

It sounds very efficient. How often do the committees meet?

Oh yes it is... The DPD meet three times per year and the sub-committees meet the month after to discuss business passed down and to pass business up for the next DPD. It means that we can generally fix most problems within three iterations allowing for amendments at committee and sub-committee levels. So allowing for amendments, urgent actions must be demonstrated as actioned in the annual report for the year following the final ratification meeting of the EFC.

Great.

Yes. And of course the audit trail is exceptionally clear. Each action of each committee and sub-committee is meticulously minuted and the fact that the minutes are cascaded bi-directionally is also minuted on receipt of the relevant minutes from lower-order and higher-order committees to which the relevant committee reports or from which minutes are received means that transparency and accountability are paramount.

Excellent. And the actual actions required and met, those are recorded in detail too?

Of course not, you see, there is a full recording of the minutes being received, read and actioned at every level, so we don't really need a record of what was actioned, that's irrelevant, we just need a record that it *was* actioned – of course, we can't be too careful, we are dealing with headroom issues related to the proposed demographic clearance after all...

Ash

Natalie Bowers

Caroline made her decision. She was better off not knowing.

She opened the car door, reached across to the passenger seat and grabbed the shoebox. Dents flattened its corners. A rubber band stretched around its middle and held down its fraying lid. Tucking it under her arm, Caroline shoved the door shut and strode around to the boot. Inside Mike's tool box, she found what she needed and headed into the woods.

The clearing was not quite how she remembered it. The trees at the edge had grown taller, but the space itself felt smaller. At five years old, she and the stumps she now towered over had been almost the same height, and her father had seemed like a giant as he had fought the policemen who were struggling to drag him off her Mum.

Her throat tightening, Caroline dropped to her knees. A bramble scraped at her hand, but she kept piling up the dry leaves. With shaking fingers, she tugged the band from the box then tossed the lid aside. The contents tumbled out, and she pulled the blowtorch from her pocket. Within seconds, every birthday card, every Christmas card her father had not been allowed to send to her, was nothing but ash.

Porcelain

Alex Thornber

At first I took her photo to show my brother the kind of girls you could find in Paris.

Tall.

Slim.

Pale skin.

Thick, long brown hair.

Permanent smile.

I fell in love with taking her photo, and her. She fell in love with having her photo taken. She always said she wanted there to be a record of her having existed. Something permanent. Light burned on negatives lasted longer than stories and memories.

After a while together, taking walks and photos, I began to notice something.

Every time I shut the shutter a small piece of her broke off and ran away. She said I must have been seeing things, looking through one eye for too long. She was fine. We carried on posing and composing photos and showing them to everyone we knew. Look at us, how fun we are, how beautiful she is, how talented I am.

I was still seeing tiny pieces of her fall off and run away. I ignored it.

Then her jeans began dragging on the floor.

"Probably lost weight, they're not sitting right on your hips," I said.

But over the weeks and months, photos and films, she shrank to the size of a frequently sharpened pencil.

I had to buy a macro lens.

I had to carry her in my shirt pocket.

She kept pleading with me to take just one more photo.

My hair looks good today.

This sunset is wonderful.

Look at my eyes sparkle.

I tried to but I couldn't resist capturing her beautiful miniature eyes on film forever.

"Just this last one," she said.

I framed her in the viewfinder and pressed the lever. I heard the shutter blades slide open, slide closed and then a tiny little explosion.

I peered from behind the camera to see my girlfriend gone, and in her place was a small pile of porcelain tiles.

The pile now sits on my bedside table, along with my camera that I haven't used since.

In her honour, every piece of my wall is plastered with photos I had taken of her. I also made duplicates and sent them to friends and family, hid them in library books, stuck them to public walls and sent them out to sea in bottles.

They are my records, along with the tiny tiles; proof that my little porcelain girlfriend existed.

Space

Valerie O'Riordan

Sally's Ma floored the milk-float down the M50. She got it up to fifteen on the hard-shoulder and she might have reached the airport if the Guards hadn't caught up with her outside Finglas. This time, the milkman pressed charges.

Sally went to see her in jail. They sat together at a small table and looked out a small window at a small dark square of sky.

Sally's Ma pointed.

—Yeh see tha' planet?

Sally looked.

—Tha's not a planet, Ma. Tha's a satellite.

—Tha's wha' I'd like. A bit a space.

—Tha's yer horse-racin' from Ascot, said Sally. Tha's yer Rangers versus Celtic. Tha's yer round-the-clock entertainment news.

Her Ma said,

—Tha's yer father talkin'.

They kept her in six weeks and released her on Sally's birthday. The three of them went as usual to Dollymount Strand, even though Sally was eighteen now and might have liked a drink. Sally's Da herded them on and off the DART. The silt of the island was tossed by the April wind and blew into their noses, their ears. Sally's Da rolled up his slacks and took wincing steps through the shallows as the drizzle started.

Sally said,

—Da, yeh don't have to.

He lifted one bare white foot from the water. Algae clung to the big toe.

—And sure what else would I do, Sal?

He carried on the paddle, his shirt spotting with rain. Sally followed him, and Sally's Ma followed her, humming a tune that the wind was fast to unpick. Thrown asunder in the thickening sky above were scraps of fabric, pieces of a rainbow dancing over Clontarf.

Sally said,

–Da. Do yeh see tha'?

–Kites, he said. Are yeh not a bit old?

–No, Da. *Tha'*.

He squinted. A dot slowly winked as the clouds swept down.

He squeezed her shoulder with a damp palm.

–Nothin' to worry abou', pet. Tha's just yer weather machine. Am I righ', Flo?

He turned. But Sally's Ma was gone. A tiny figure rushed the dunes. Between the hillocks they saw the bright side of an ice-cream truck heading for the bridge. Sally's Da began to run.

Mauve

Carrie Etter

I opened the door to see my ex-girlfriend Tricia, holding a purplish object the size of a football. It looked like papier-mâché.

"What's that?" I asked. I wasn't about to invite her in.

She smiled. "The apology you wanted."

"A bit late, don't you think?" I said.

She shrugged as her smile slipped away. "I thought you'd still want it."

"Well, yes—"

"It took me a lot of work," she added.

"Really," I said, bending forward to survey it more closely.

"In fact, it's taken me *all* this time to make it."

"All this time? It took you three months to make *that*?"

She glared and drew the apology to her chest. "If you don't appreciate it—"

"Hang on," I said softly. "I didn't say that."

She sniffed and held the apology more tightly. As seconds passed, her grasp seemed to relax, and gingerly I put my hand on it. She made the smallest gasp, but remained still. I began to see in the apology's mauve the iridescence of tears, which, in the right light, gave the object an opalescent sheen. I wondered what to say next, how to coax it away from her. I wanted that apology, and damned if I wasn't going to have it.

Superman

L.A. Craig

A woman I've not really seen before and am not seeing now, sits by my desk. She tells me of night sweats, dryness down there, her worry of thinning bones. She says she's not interested in replacing any hormones. Can I offer anything else? Trust me I'm a doctor, I want to say, HRT's your best bet, but she's full of the side effects she found on the internet.

Her notes tell me I saw her in July. Conjunctivitis. I try to remember, imagine her sitting there dressed for summer, but it doesn't come. She spots the photograph of Simon at Chessington, says her grandson has the same T-shirt, *Superman mad he is.*

"No more problems with your eyes then?" I ask her.

She looks on the point of being insulted.

"Conjunctivitis," I say.

"Oh, I'm with you," she says. "No, the drops did the trick."

Then she goes all holistic on me: fruit cake recipes, St John's Wort, soya this and that. I say I sympathise but there's no concrete medical evidence. I'll write the prescription anyway, in case she changes her mind.

She shakes her head. "I wish you'd bloody listen."

"Look, Mrs..." I glance at the monitor.

"Jagger. Not that difficult to remember. Like Dagger. Shagger. Shag her. You fancy that?"

"Mrs Jagger, I really don't think..."

"Woke you up though didn't it? Not that I could manage it mind you, chafes you see, like I said, dried up."

I imagine her naked. A mnemonic I won't forget next time.

"I can give you something to ease that." I add to the prescription, but she doesn't seem to hear. She's in her handbag, pulls out a purse that's not much smaller and points to a boy inside the plastic window.

"Darren," she says. "Looks about the same age as yours."

I lean in, like I'm interested. The boy is wearing the same Superman T-shirt.

"How's Darren doing at school?" I ask.

"Oh he does all right, plenty of cheek on him mind you," and then she's off on some rant about him being just like his granddad. I turn, begin to type up her notes.

"If that's everything, Mrs Jagger?"

She's in her bag again. "There is *one* other thing."

"Mm hm?" I say, eyes still on the screen.

Next thing I know she's grabbed my left wrist and manacled it to the desk leg with fluffy pink handcuffs.

"Mood swings," she says. "One minute I'm fine, the next I'm that green monster with the shredded shirt, hair a right mess."

She's in my face, hirsute upper lip. It glistens, but I have no authority to persuade her that this might also benefit from HRT.

"Sorry love," she nods towards the handcuffs, "but you stopped listening." She slumps, goes quiet. Now she has my attention, it seems she doesn't know what to do next.

I need to save us both more embarrassment.

"So, where's Superman when you need him?" I ask.

She shrugs. "Washing his tights?"

Home

Calum Kerr

Dominic paused outside the apartment, his head hanging. He breathed deeply for a moment, then straightened his shoulders, lifted his head, put his key in the lock and went in.

"Hi honey, I'm home!" he called.

Sally emerged from the kitchen, wiping her wet hands on her apron. He stepped up to kiss her, but the smile fell from her face and she pulled away from him. "What is it?" she asked.

He opened his mouth, but nothing came out.

"You've found it, haven't you?"

He met her gaze for a moment, but then his resolve crumbled. His nod left him staring at the floor.

She stepped close and put her hand out. She rested it on his shoulder which rose and fell in a sob.

"Yes," he said. "I didn't... uh... I didn't mean to. But I went to the store and it was just there."

"The store? Al's? But you've been there so many times before."

He shook his head. "I know. There's no science to these things. They appear wherever. They don't last long, either." She saw tears and anguish in his eyes and wanted to wrap her arms around him, but she had her own hurt to nurse. "You know all this," he said, an accusation in his voice. "We talked about it so often."

"So, that's it, then? You're going home? You've found your door and you're going to go back where you came from?"

"I –" he started.

"I thought we'd talked about it. I thought you were happy here. I thought you loved me enough to give up that world, that future, that hell, and stay here with me."

He pulled out from under her hand and turned into the kitchen. He grabbed the bottle of bourbon and poured himself a shot. She walked in behind him.

"What happened, Dom? What happened to all the things we said?"

He turned back. "I never thought I'd find it. It had already been two years when I met you. I'd never been stuck through a door for that long. I thought I'd missed my slot. I thought this was it."

He closed the distance between them.

"And I was glad. I found you. And I love you. And the future could look after itself! I didn't want to go!"

"But now you've found it, and, that's it, you're off?!"

He put his drink down and took her hands. "Come with me!" he implored her.

She pulled free. "We talked about this, Dom. There's no way I want to be part of that hard, harsh world you've described! You go if you have to, but I'm staying right here."

She turned and walked out of the kitchen, leaving him staring at the empty door. He retrieved his drink and moved to the window. He drank in sips and stared out at the past.

He stood and watched the sky grow dark. When he reached the bottom of the glass, he poured another.

Beauty

Kylie Grant

I am watching my house burn. The October wind is strong and forces my head up so that I'm unable to look away; wood bends and splinters, glass breaks, and tiles from the roof slide with ease and land with a dull thud on the sodden lawn. Amongst it all is the fire; flicks of orange, a haze of black around the edges, tear through the living room, breathing life into a room so often still at this time of day. I am stood at the gate, one hand still on the rusted metal entrance, the other holding the flowers for my wife. My wife, the woman who has set our house ablaze. I made sure not to buy carnations, carnations my mother had told me, were for liars and secretaries, buy a woman a tulip instead, she had told me, tulips are for women who want love but don't need it.

I can hear the sea, can hear it breaking and drawing back and can taste the salt on my tongue. It is one of the reasons why I persuaded my wife to move here. I like to imagine all of the people who have tasted the same air, bitten down on the same grains of sand, and felt the whip of salty residue left by the wind. I told my wife that I needed to be closer to the factory, the commute was too long and too dull, and so we had moved from a placid suburb to a house that withstood the elements, a house that knew its place. It wasn't only the sea though. It was Ella.

Ella has a body that women pull their hair out for, a body that wears clothes like a second skin. Before Ella I designed mannequins; plastic and breathless, soulless, heart-less and sexless. Since her, I am an artist. I sculpt bodies that you all want, desire, and purchase at any cost; you buy her, you buy from her, and you buy because of her. She is what really led me here, to this dead town, to the endless sounds of the sea.

Yesterday my wife caught us. She caught me smoothing

wet, grey plaster over Ella's body; caught Ella's satisfied squeal and my laugh. She hurled mannequin limbs at us both. Ella bled large drops of crimson blood onto the white lino.

Now I stand in front of my glowing house. My wife must have set fire to the mannequins first, they lay piled up on the front lawn. The plastic has melted, merging them together into a congealed shapeless mass, swelling and deflating like the undulating surface of the sea, and for a moment all that I desire is to swim into its depths, far down, where perfect beauty lies still in the darkness.

Harps

Sal Page

It was my idea to start the orchestra. Up until then whenever we met up we just chatted. On and on. About the weather, children, husbands, parents, spring cleaning, the garden, meals cooked and meals eaten. Conversations that went round and round in circles, endlessly repeating ourselves and getting nowhere.

Now we chat for only a few minutes until a natural hush falls over the group. We know it's time. We stand up - the only sound the occasional chair scrape. We arrange ourselves on the church hall stage, each chair at the same angle and spaced out at intervals of exactly two and a half feet. We sit with our knees a relaxed distance apart, heads raised, necks loosened, hair shook out free behind. We pause for a few seconds looking out across our invisible audience. We smile. We breathe. We move our arms, elbows slightly akimbo, bingo wings flapping.

We play our invisible harps and forget all the details of our lives outside this hall and sometimes I can even hear the music we make.

Camembert

Jonathan Pinnock

When I answered the door, it was just after eleven o'clock on a bright night full of stars. She took off her helmet and shook her head so that her silver-blonde hair sparkled with the light of the moon.

"Hello?" I said.

She held out some kind of container. "Do you have fuel? For my spaceship?"

I didn't.

"That's a shame," she said, pushing past me. "I'll have to stay over then. Do you have cheese? I like cheese."

I did.

She stayed for three months. The sex was relentless and at times quite unusual. But in the end I got bored.

"What's wrong?" she said, stroking my chest.

"This isn't working," I said, moving her hand away.

"Why not?"

"We have nothing in common."

"So?"

I sighed. "And I'm sick of the way you keep going on about all the other planets you've visited. Makes me feel inadequate."

"I – "

"Also, the cheese thing is a bit weird." She'd made me buy a new fridge just to keep all the different varieties in. Why were there so many? I'd never really seen the problem with Cathedral City.

"I – "

"And finally, I don't think you've even got a spaceship."

Well, I was wrong there.

We spent the next three months touring the galaxy. We watched the twin moons rise over the planet Xhorbius 29. We flew in figures of eight around the neon geysers of Bhatharrghul Minor. We skimmed over the perpetual rolling earthquakes that scarred the surface of Klatcharquasatch VI beta.

I quite liked the zero gravity sex, too.

But all was not well.

"What's wrong?" I said, running my hand down her spine.

"This isn't working," she said, pushing herself away from me.

"Why not?"

"You're boring."

"What?" I couldn't believe this. I'd pandered to her every need. I'd even lugged that sodding fridge of hers all the way over to where she'd hidden her spaceship. We still hadn't run out of cheese, either.

"Everywhere we go, all you can ever think of saying is 'Wow, that's amazing!' or 'Cor, brilliant!' or 'Whoa!' You have no imagination, that's your problem."

I couldn't think of anything to say.

She dumped me. Unfortunately, we were too far away from Earth for her to dump me anywhere near my home. However, to be fair, she did at least dump me on a planet with a reasonably well-developed ecosystem and not too many predatory species. The climate is generally pretty favourable and there is plenty to eat. I've built myself a nice, comfortable shelter and I've even just about got used to the twenty-hour diurnal cycle.

The odd thing is, it's the cheese I miss the most. I'd give anything for a wedge of Camembert.

Summertime

Susan F. Giles

You lie together, close enough to hear each other breathing but not quite touching. The rough meadow grass scratches at your bare shoulders and you'll have a rash there tonight.

'I'm too old for this,' you tell the smoke that curls above your head. Cassie shuffles beside you, her legs rustling against the grass as she sits up.

'Too old for what?' she asks, as if it isn't obvious – as if you aren't sat in a field, smoking in the mid-summer sun.

'For sitting in a field, getting stoned,' you reply with more than a little bite, 'for wasting my whole summer, sitting in a field getting stoned.'

Fingers barely touch yours as she reaches for the joint, and there is silence as she inhales and holds. Above you, a butterfly skitters across the sky and if you tried, you could reach out and touch it, catch the curve of its creamy wings with the tip of your finger.

'What else should we be doing?' Cassie's words rush out with the smoke, 'Studying? Working? Growing up, growing old?'

Yes, you think, turning to watch as she takes another drag; leaves a small translucent ring on the paper. She offers it back, waves the damp end in your direction. You consider it for a moment, then you dismiss it with a shake of your head, 'Anything – we should be doing something!'

'We are,' she smiles at you, squinting against the sun and her expression is almost cruel. 'We're wasting our summer sitting in a field.'

Wrapped

Martha Williams

Mary runs into shops.

"My name is Mary, my name is Mary!" she cries, louder and louder, spinning around. The daisies on her skirt fly. The grass seeds in her hair spill down. The brightness of her catches them, one by one, 'til they all look.

There are chocolates.

Mary sees them, walks up and stops, tippy-toe solemn, and presses her finger against the purple, red, and silver foil wrappers. She pauses, silent. She sticks out her lips to make her pokey-bum-mouth, and rolls her eyes sideways until they catch someone in particular. She always tries to find someone very, very old.

Very, very old people like Mary, they say, "Here's ten pee."

And she says, "It's fifteen pee."

And they say, "Well then, young Mary, here's another five pee." And when she buys her chocolate she gives them her choccy-sucky missing-tooth grin and waves, and they say, "Aw." As if they remember being a bit like Mary or having someone a bit like Mary of their own. Then Mary skips away with chocolate in her mouth and the day all warm on her back.

If she catches a young person, they smile too, but they don't give out ten pee or fifteen pee and there's no chocolate in them.

And grown-ups with children of their own are rubbish and never ever give out anything, because they ask questions like, "Where's your Mummy?" Then Mary's smile falls off and her face becomes see-through, like the plastic wrapped around the raw meat in the freezer aisle.

Natural

Sarah-Clare Conlon

Mr Green puts the green in greengrocer. His juicy Coxes loll in wicker baskets; his dirty carrots nestle in wooden boxes.

"Nothing wrong with a bit of muck," he says so often his wife repeats it in her sleep.

Still, she will admit they've not been able to keep the tweedy types away since branching out into seasonal, organic and local. "No airmiles here, eh Mrs Green?" he informs them, via her, at least twice a day.

No funny carpet tile patches of fake grass, either. No tacky plastic frames with interchangeable digits. No orange and lime starbursts. Mr Green's displays are pared down, and he's particularly proud of the slate plant markers he daubs prices onto with special chalk.

All it takes is a damp cloth and a cocked eyebrow for Mrs Green to wipe away the rogue apostrophes. It wouldn't do for the *Guardian* readers to spot them.

Ciphers

Eli Goldstone

Well, they were love letters. I mean it basically just amounted to a list of things that I'd seen being thrown out around the village. I wrote whenever I saw something, and in between writing I'd pray that somewhere somebody was putting something out on the street so that I could write to him about it.

I remember everything. A Moses basket. It was a really warm evening and I also saw a man in a suit walking down the road singing opera tunelessly to himself. Or rather, he was singing opera tunelessly to everybody. The sky was blushing. You know the kind of evening I mean. The Moses basket had a note attached to it. Sometimes people do that. 'Please take me', that kind of thing. 'One loose handle'. A cast iron milk pan with a little burn on the bottom. I took that home. I hung it from a hook in my kitchen. A couple of wine racks tied together with string. The objects were ciphers. I wrote to him, I said 'A couple of wine racks tied together with string', but what I was trying to communicate was, 'Hey, I love you, and I have run out of new ways to say that'.

I never have had the knack for saying the things that I've wanted to say. I remember one of the first nights we were together. He was standing in my bedroom and I was sort of drunk. He was in front of my bookshelves judging me like that, you know, touching the spines, making little surprised noises. We'd been kissing on my bed. I was tidying my hair. He laughed at my Jenna Jameson autobiography and looked at me. You know, like, 'What?'

I said, "She taught me everything I know about sucking dick."

I mean. That's really what I said.

So eventually I started thinking, does he know? Does he read about a foot spa with an exposed cable and think, 'These things are her way of making sense of being completely dulled by the dogged enormity of her obsession with me'? And if he doesn't think that, does it matter? Is the important thing that I mean the thing that I say or that the thing that I say is interpreted correctly? What is the important thing?

I don't know. I don't know.

I saw a table today. It had been dismantled so the top was missing, so that it was really just four legs held together by a hole. I thought, 'Is that a table?' You know, the old how many rocks make a pile etcetera. I thought, that would be interesting, to write to him about that. To dedicate three pages of semiotics to the clandestine pursuit of his heart. For a moment, I just stood there, thinking that.

Marmite

David R. Morgan

I open my jar of marmite and there he is; there is Jesus. The Lord manifests in so many ways. I have an oven that makes a different sound every hour. Sometimes it sings like a choir; sometimes slow, solemn as a Liturgy. At least once a day it is a peal of bells; a church service from medieval times. I fry baked beans on its ceramic hobs. My new pet *Hallelujah* is a giant flea; it has little prayer dogs running around on it. I eat for love; seeking substance and meaning. I make a sandwich of fried baked beans and marmite. I'm not particularly religious but I like to think Jesus is looking out for us. At the back of my larder there is a door that runs from floor to ceiling; one day I'll open it up and, amen, walk through.

Elsewhere

Alison Wells

"No-body told me you were dead," she said to the corpse in the ante-room.

Constance had received a letter from him that morning making plans for his return. It was as if there were two of him, the man in the coffin and the other, still in London, writing her letters.

He was old fashioned that way. He liked to put things on paper. "For the record. In case anything happens to me." He lived as if he'd expected to be famous, as if it was only a matter of time. Constance preferred the phone, even though Daniel thought it didn't do well in getting to the essence of the person.

At that controversial exhibition years ago: human cadavers presented, dissected for education and aesthetics. Some of the bodies were said to be unclaimed, as if no-one knew they were gone – although they were now seen by thousands. She'd held Daniel's hand so tight. That night, she pressed her body against the span of him. He'd moved to London to lie low from thrown suspicions: something about his brother and a missing friend, who showed up, years later, perfectly fine.

She remembered how she'd woken up this morning to the radio: a news item about someone found dead in his armchair beside the Christmas tree. In March. Later, a phone call from her husband Malcolm; the car's battery was kaput, could she pick him up for lunch? And in between, the letter, if she could keep it all straight in her head.

It was so strange. She had called to the funeral home purely to deliver flowers but no-one was about. She'd stepped into the ante-room then saw him, Daniel there, dead.

"Untimely," murmured the undertaker, arriving. "He was returning from London. He'd been on his way to the airport."

"But his relations?" Constance asked, glancing around. The man shrugged, closed the coffin. Constance could no longer see Daniel, in her mind's eye, lying there.

In the car Malcolm was stoney silent, his outline stark against the fickle flickering of Spring.

As they swung along a familiar road, she remembered her father, now long gone, telling her about a night watchman dead for weeks before anyone noticed because someone had lit the light nightly in the watchman's hut. And there again, at this corner, by the library, Constance had once seen her mother on the street, before she realised it couldn't be her.

She had lunch with Malcolm, gazpacho and cold prawns. It all seemed inconsequential. She drove home through the constant dappling of leaves.

In the house the sunlight tried to enter through the net curtains. She took out her writing pad and answered Daniel's letter. A week later she received a reply in his handwriting. No phone call, of course – not his style. The letters kept coming, in typical Daniel fashion. Everything was as before. Constance imagined him in London among the bright red buses and the life.

Shed

SJI Holliday

There's a man in the shed. He has paintbrush hair; his eyes are balls of twine. His torso is a stack of paint cans; his arms are long-handled brooms. He has no legs. He sits at the back, on the shelf, beside the bottles of white spirit and the badly wound extension cord and the toolbox with nothing inside. The tools are all in the house; the hammer is missing. Screwdrivers are in kitchen drawers beside dishwasher stained cutlery and paper packets of chopsticks from the local Chinese. The shed stays locked most of the time. Like the back door. We don't go in the garden now. The lawn is hidden by black bags full of things. Things we need but we can't keep in the shed anymore; or the house. Broken lawnmowers, an old television, piles of papers that need to be burned. Food for the cats. Umbrellas turned inside out. People come round sometimes, but we send them away. Sometimes we don't answer the door.

Bar

Nicholas Murray

She said she was a sword swallower.

A dying art if I ever heard of one.

At first I was in disbelief. When I came over I expected something more ordinary. Not too ordinary mind you, she was too intriguing to be an accountant or a tax collector. A visual puzzle, displaying her own impossibility. To be honest, I didn't know what I was expecting, but it wasn't *that*. I gave her a sceptical smirk, a silent challenge that she accepted without so much as a breath. With thumb and forefinger she pulled the swizzle stick from her gin and tonic.

Her throat rippled as she tilted her head back. Preparations? Nerves? Maybe she wasn't a sword swallower at all. Maybe she was regretting the bluff now that I'd called her on it. Her neck was pale and flawless. Almost luminescent in the carefully planned gloom of the bar.

With the tender languorous speed of a performer; slow enough to show that what she was about to do was in no way easy, but with enough speed to make sure I knew exactly how much confidence she placed in her skill, she touched end of stick to tip of tongue.

From there it slid slowly back. Then down.

For a few seconds she was a painted statue. Motionless, with her hand to her mouth, two fingers missing. I stared, another gaping fool at one of her shows.

As she pulled it back out from the depths of her throat I caught a glimpse of the inside of her cheek. Perhaps that was all part of the act too, deftly considered to the very end. It was patterned with a frantic stripework of scars.

The swizzle was placed on the bar, cutting the square of a napkin in two. She looked at me with an indecipherable half-smile.

"So, what do *you* do?"

Waterman

Eunice Yeates

It lay in two lonely halves on the kitchen table and by the time Hannah understood the issue it was too late. The gel ink refill was wrong for the Waterman; Vincent's Christmas present to her. She strained to remove the cartridge and swore obscenely when it gave, leaving part of itself deep inside the pen's cavity. Nothing she did would extract it now.

Silly to cry over such a thing, but slow tears insisted still. Midnight blue with silver trim, it had looked so sleek and elegant in its presentation case. Hannah liked slipping it from under the leather tab and feeling its heft in her hand, maybe swirling a small design on the back of an envelope, or stylising her signature.

Before the refill (which was included in the gift bag) caused all the trouble, the pen's first assignment was to be a thank-you card for Vincent. Aggrieved, Hannah turned its cushioned box over in her hands and, by chance, discovered a warranty under the Waterman's bed. It had a stamp from the department store, a handwritten date and an original signature: L. Bentley. Hannah put her coat on.

At the glass counter she was greeted by a dapper gent with 'Maurice' on the name badge pinned to his waistcoat. Like a surgeon, he peered down his bifocals as she showed him the debacle in two parts. Maurice stopped with a start when he saw the decapitated refill.

'This is a Parker refill,' he cried, appalled. 'Your pen takes *Waterman* refills; nothing else. Plus it is ballpoint ONLY. No gel!'

'I tried in good faith to insert the refill that was sold with the pen,' Hannah said softly. Then she produced the warranty, which he accepted, adjusting his spectacles.

'Bentley,' he spat, with practiced disdain.

Maurice took a Swiss Army Knife from his trouser-pocket and jousted at the wedged item. Nothing. He switched blades and worked at it some more. Hannah noticed that, in his zeal, he had slightly damaged her pen. Evidently he saw it too.

'I'll telephone the boss,' he said.

He depressed the digits with the base of a Sheaffer and waited, foot-tapping, then hung up. He tried again and this time got through. Hannah only heard scraps of the exchange: Sorry to bother you... Before Christmas... Waterman... Lorna Bentley... Customer attempted to force a Parker refill...

'Well, I was just trying the refill you provided,' Hannah chimed in quickly.

Then Lorna Bentley materialised, apparently from her lunch break.

'What's going on?' she asked nobody in particular, and nobody replied.

'Yes, right, OK, yes,' Maurice was saying into the receiver, then he ended the call.

Taking in the items on the counter, Lorna suddenly exclaimed, 'Yikes, did I sell a Parker refill with a Waterman?'

Maurice ignored her.

'We're giving you a new pen,' he said to Hannah, officiously.

Hannah left Maurice and Lorna in the soup of their mutual dislike and skipped up the escalator, relieved and pleased.

Troll

Nick Garrard

In the wood is a house and in the house, another wood. Saplings have burst through the floor and spread their roots across the carpet. Vines dress the walls like wires. You may think it has been left to rot but this house is not empty. A troll lives here. He has dark hair and blue eyes and stubble. He sits around all day in a t-shirt and pyjamas, looking out of the windows and moving silently between floors. He is kept there by a spell which makes passing through the doorway agony. He might never leave.

Once, a little girl came to the house selling biscuits. She had blonde hair in bunches and a smile fixed right in the middle of her face. The troll remembers the way she looked up as he cautiously peeled the door open. She didn't turn and run into the woods. She didn't burst into tears. She stayed exactly where she stood and held out a box in hands as white as willow. He bought the biscuits and ate them slowly, one by one, sitting in his armchair. He watched the girl move off into the day, skipping softly down the garden path. The saplings began to stir in the afternoon breeze.

Boy

Jay Barnett

They say it's a young boy, always at one end of a corridor, no face as such.

I fix lights, fan coil units, make sure passive infrared systems pick up movement. On a few occasions I have to enter the box. It's more concert hall than box but that's what we call it anyway. They put them to sleep then send us in with fifteen to twenty guards armed with harpoons, high powered carbine rifles, sometimes even bazookas.

All just to fix a light bulb.

One weekend I was there alone working overtime. I was peering from the observation deck down into the box. They move so fast.

It left a trail of web thick as I am tall clinging to everything. The crane bots moved out to scrape away the webbing, they fed it down their pipes to the cellars for processing.

I turned around and down at the other end of the corridor was a young boy, no face as such.

Of all the places to be haunted.

Rapture

Kirsty Logan

1.

It's because of the boys my momma says, and she sure would
know because she's had more than anyone: lined up along the
fence they were, noon till dusk, hats in their hands and shoes
scuffing the dirt. That's what everyone says, and everyone
knows everyone here. And me? I sure know lots of boys.
Momma says church camp is for girls to make good, but I
know there will be enough boys to share: a different one every
day, behind the kitchen annex, breath sticky and dicks hard as
marbles.

2.

Sacred Heart's basement smells of stewed broccoli and boy-
sweat and air-con and drugstore body-spray. The pastor says
welcome and forgive, then it's on to praising and stomping,
singing and fainting: just in time for damnation. *It's the girls*,
says the pastor, *snake-charmers, hypnotists, bellies of sin! You keep
away*, he says, and I wonder just how I'm supposed to keep
away from myself. *The end is coming*, he says, *repent repent before
it's too late REPENT SINNERS AND SERPENTS*. The sky
rumbles in a threat of thunder, and then it's not the sky but
the world, the world and us
> the walls the floor the roof
> shake shudder howl rearrange
and we're screaming we're crying the world is ending and so
are we and I repent oh lord I repent I'm sorry I am a sinner I
am a serpent but I repent I respond I repose I am yours I'll
never I'll never again –

3.

At school I find out that a parent suggested the end of the world would purge our sins. The church camp counsellors dropped tables on the floor of the dining room over the basement. Two weeks after the end of the world, I go behind the school cafeteria with a new boy. I know whose parent gets the danger of sin. *It's because of your momma,* the boys all say.

Buttons

Kevlin Henney

Pint in one hand. Clasped. Wouldn't want it to go to waste. Key card in the other. Got it ready. Mustn't look drunk.

Marjorie waited, swaying gently, no breeze but the air-conditioning.

Was the lift slow? Or was it just relative to the evening's rapid flow of drinks? Gerry, the MD, had wrapped up the sales-and-management awayday hours earlier. It was straight into the G-and-Ts, followed by the margaritas, followed by the nameless alcopops, followed by beer, wine and more beer. Food? She remembered peanuts.

Leaving the bar had been a good call. She'd had a few too many. If she didn't get back to her room she was worried the next one would be a co-worker not a drink. She'd sensed she was overflirting, practically groping her male colleagues, undressing them with her throaty laugh. Their beer goggles filling with expectation, slowly restoring her to youth. They were looking at her — to her — not just at the pretty young things — the bitches — from reception and purchasing.

Fuck. She'd dropped her key card. Bending over — more revealing than she'd meant to be, but not as easy as it used to be — she saw two buttons undone on her blouse. Did that happen earlier or just now? More revealing than she'd meant to be.

Ting. The lift door closed in front of her as she stood up. Fuck. She hadn't heard it arrive. She pressed the button. Too late. More waiting. At least she had a drink and yet another reason to have it.

Affairs as short as they were doomed. Drunken one-nighters with younger men whose regret she saw across the pillow in the morning. Or older men who couldn't believe their luck but couldn't get it up. At least tonight she'd be taking only the drink to her room.

Her marriage had limped across the finishing line twenty years after a false start. A husband whose long-running deceit had fooled her and three other women, an extended family she never knew she had. A son who drifted everywhere and committed to nothing, from his iPod shuffle to his carousel of girlfriends. A daughter whose prudishness seemed a studied response to her family, distancing herself by more than a reasonable airfare.

All gone. All done. Alone.

"Mar-jo-rie!" Jack sang her name across the foyer. "Looking good. How's it going?" He walked towards her, tie loose, shirt untucked, top two buttons undone, beer bottle in hand and a confident swagger that steered clear of a straight line. But a smile all for her.

Ting. She caught the door. They got in.

"Floor?" Jack's hands waved in front of the panel, nimble, conjuring, charming, drunken.

"Top floor, Jack." Smile. "All the way."

He pressed all the buttons, all the right buttons. The lift was slow. Jack was quick. But, at least tonight, she'd be taking only the drink to her room.

Cheese

David Gilbert

I.

She says I have used too much of the remaining cheese for my sandwiches - the same cheese that she had left for Adam's sandwiches. I say *there's plenty of cheese left for his sandwiches and I haven't used too much for mine. And even if I have,* I say, *I can give you back a slice for his or even more. But I'm sure there's plenty of cheese for both our sandwiches.* She says there isn't enough for both our sandwiches and she should know, her being the one who usually makes his sandwiches. I put quite a big slice of cheese aside on a plate and say *there you are. I've put some cheese on the plate for him.* I am about to put another slice of cheese on the plate, just in case, but decide that's going too far. Then I notice that the slice of cheese I have put on the plate has pickle on it so I wipe that off while she is not looking. He doesn't like pickle on his cheese sandwiches. That much I do know.

II.

On reading the above, she asks how I had wiped the pickle off the cheese. Was it with a knife? Was it clean or dirty? Knowing you, she says, it was probably with your finger. *It wasn't with my finger,* I say remembering what I had used to wipe the pickle off the cheese. So what was it? she says. *Kitchen towel,* I say. She goes to brush her teeth. It's feasible, I think, looking round to see if I can spot the roll of kitchen towel and whether it could feasibly have been nearby at the time. But there is no roll of kitchen towel. It must have run out yesterday. I fetch a new roll of kitchen towel from the hall cupboard, tear off a few sheets, so it doesn't look quite so new and place it between the fridge and bread board before she comes back in.

Boom

Simon Thirsk

What Fanny May liked most about university was shopping, and the helpful way that everyone she did business with made life easy for her and explained things in such simple and straightforward terms.

Buying with Mummy's consummate skill, she once found three £5 packets of smoked salmon for the price of one. Her receipt informed her that she had saved £10, which – even if you deducted the £5 she had spent - was still a £5 profit. "But why should you deduct the £5," her flatmates – all arts students – reasoned, "when all three of us have a £5 packet?"

After that they all began saving money in this brilliant new way. And Fanny kept a monthly record of their savings, which was often several hundred pounds a term between them, counting the happy hours, free entry to nightclubs and miscellaneous special offers.

Fanny became quite famous in her faculty, which was, of course, economics. And then in the whole university.

She understood perfectly that nothing is for nothing in this world so when she went to work in the City of London she gave her first year's work absolutely free – being an intern, they called it – but that was more than offset by the £5,000 cashback on her car and the rent-free first quarter on the lease of her riverside flat.

It was soon obvious that the lessons she had learned at university had given her a magic touch. Not only did she find innovative ways of saving, she found even more imaginative ways of marketing her savings schemes, enabling people to save in ways they had never saved before.

The more they borrowed, the more they saved. And the more they saved, the more they had to invest, especially in houses and land. As Fanny told them: "Obviously, no one can make more land – so prices can only rise. Just buy."

So they did.

And they did.

And the more people spent, the more they saved. And the more the shops and shoppers, and manufacturers, banks and shareholders – and everyone! – prospered. Fanny even found brilliant new ways to borrow money herself to use to lend – so people could save even more.

And the whole world prospered like never before. In fact, even when they had invested the money she had borrowed and lent them (and no one could believe this), she found ways to sell their debts and hedge their risks to invest again and become even richer.

Everyone loved their mortgages, loans, credit cards and pensions. And their purchases. And how house prices rose, and pensions grew.

And they simply adored how they could buy whatever they wanted for only the cost of the interest. And even take out another loan, if necessary, to pay that.

How they laughed and applauded her environmentalism when Fanny explained how she had recycled their pension funds, mortgages and credit cards back to them yet again.

Why the world economy suddenly collapsed, they had absolutely no idea.

Celia

Sue Walker-Stokes

Twenty miles from Exeter the car began to shudder. Clouds of steam shot up through the shiny red bonnet onto the windscreen, blinding them both.

'Christ!' Ted instinctively braked and swung into the verge.

They were on a quiet stretch of country road. Peggy lay back against the sun-warmed black leather seats and silently fumed. *Bloody typical.* A 'fun' trip from one end of this grey, rain-sodden country to the other. This most definitely wasn't her idea of a celebration. A flight to a Mediterranean island would have been a far better way to celebrate thirty years of marriage.

But Peggy knew that the damned car would be involved. Ted doted on it, or Celia as he called it. He'd bought the Chevrolet six months after their wedding. The primary object of his affections, thought Peggy wryly.

Ted stuck his head over the bonnet, silver strands of hair sticking up weirdly and his glasses all steamed up. *What a silly looking sod. I don't know why I stuck with him so long.* Actually she did know. It was the money. It was a huge turn-on. Bless him. The thought of it still cheered her up.

The sound of a fast approaching car jolted her back in the moment. A white Porsche was slowing down and then braked thirty yards down the road. A man jumped out and jogged up to them.

'Do you guys need any help?'

Immediately, Peggy recognised him. *My God - Tony. He'd hardly changed. The sex had been great.* When was it? One of her first conquests, not long after the boring honeymoon.

Peggy reddened and dropped her chin, looking up coquettishly. He gave her a friendly nod and disappeared behind the bonnet.

He doesn't recognise me. The little shit. Do I look that old? She folded her arms and turned away, listening to the men bonding over Celia's engine parts.

Her eyes drifted over to the sports car. A woman sat in the passenger seat. Timid, mousey, undistinguished-looking. The woman was looking intently. *At what?* Peggy followed her gaze and settled on – Ted. He had also seen the woman and stopped in mid-sentence. Their eyes locked. Peggy froze and there was a silence.

Tony's oil-smeared face popped up and he looked over at the woman in the sports car.

'Nearly done. Have you got a tissue, Celia?'

Elephant

Erinna Mettler

Ella watched through prison bars. Mrs Blinkinsop gave them the facts in a disinterested voice,

'...up to 15,000 pounds...tons of vegetation...very poor hearing...'

Ella took a donut from her lunchbox and bit into it.

The boys laughed. She could sense one of them behind her (probably Jacob Kent) puffing out his cheeks and waddling from side to side.

'...critically endangered... up to seventy years...no natural predators...'

Ella bit again, sticking her tongue into the volcanic jam at the centre, and felt that familiar moment of security.

A bun flew past her ear and hit the animal's mud-crackled hide.

'...prehensile nose. And now onto the tigers. Mr Kent you can walk with me. Ella it is not lunchtime; it is not even elevenses, put the donut away.'

Ella froze.

'God she's so disgusting,' said Imelda Wilkinson to one of her friends. She knocked Ella with her shoulder as she went past, 'enjoying the family re-union Nelly?'

Ella didn't follow the class. She took another bite and watched a tear glisten on grey wrinkles. Birds twittered on the incarcerated trees and a little door opened in Ella's brain. She saw the history of the world contained in that single globe of pachyderm distress. The fury of Victor at the battle of Heraclea, Hannibal's triumphant crossing, the march of Claudius into Colchester, Charlemagne's beloved Abul-Abbas, Alexander's army, the temples of Mysore, the menagerie at The Tower, Castor and Pollux roasted and eaten at the siege of Paris, Raja, who carried the Buddha's tooth in a casket on

his back, Orwell's shotgun conscience, endless feathered head
-dresses and cracked whips. Ella saw all these triumphs and
humiliations in one tear.

She looked down at her donut, the ragged fleshy tooth-
mark and the oozing jam, and tossed it into the bin. She
rubbed her fingers on the front of her dress, patted down her
hair and took the first steps on her voyage to vicious
dictatorship.

Bee

Emma J. Lannie

Ow. The sting is a shock. The bee drops to the windowsill. I examine the heel of my palm where the stinger is still attached. The image of my hand spread against the net curtains, and the bee, will stay with my small daughter for all of her life.

There is so much sadness in this room. The bee lies dead on the windowsill. My hand throbs. It is a wonder to me that I can feel anything. My husband is somewhere else. There are other rooms to be emptied, closed down. He is in one of them, and I hope that he has found the space to cry, to own his sadness.

This is just a house now. The room where my daughter played shop, with tins emptied from cupboards, is just a room. My husband's mother will never again swap pennies for tins of mandarin segments. I will be the one to play this game with my daughter from now on, but my efforts will be hurried and brief, bookended by feeds and changing nappies and trying to figure out what I am doing with my life.

My husband's mother loved me like a daughter. When she came to stay, it was underwritten with the idea that she would come back here, when she was better.

The stinger is not lodged deep. I scrape it out with my fingernail. There is baking soda in the kitchen cupboard still, and I make a paste with water and apply it to the sting. My daughter clings to my legs, her arms wrapped tight around my thighs. I reassure her I am okay.

This is difficult to do with her here. My husband wanted to leave her at my sister's, with the baby, but yesterday she called me a liar. When we got here this morning, she knocked on the door while my husband struggled with the key. I don't know what rules govern the dead, but knocking before you enter their home is a good politeness, I think. Something I would also have done, had I been here alone. Once the door was open, she darted inside, shouting, "Nana" into every room. My husband stalled at the door. I went in, my heart in pieces.

All rooms exhausted, my daughter came to me slow, defeated. This was the only place she thought her Nana could be. I lifted her. She wrapped her limbs tight around me.

I know you're supposed to keep these things from children. But my daughter is four years old and wiser than the lot of us.

We go back into the front room. She rests her chin on the windowsill and whispers to the bee. I don't hear what she says. I take the nets down and my daughter helps me fold them, our arms wide, our hands coming together in a dance that is all about the lives of women. A dance that is also a kind of prayer.

Blackhole

Jessica Patient

The view from my home isn't postcard perfect. There are
shadows, always. I used to manage my land-locked hotel, ideal
for romantic weekend breaks, and keep chickens as a hobby.
Now, my house sits on the edge of a crumbling cliff and
stares out to a micro blackhole. I am out of sync.

A scientist in his kitchenette created the blackhole while
his flatmates watched re-runs of *Star Trek*. An eruption of
panic buying, clogged roads and raging riots happened when
the containment field failed. Every building devoured by the
blackhole was considered breaking news. I became obsessed
with the news channel. In the beginning I stayed up for
seventy-two hours. The blackhole gradually consumed the city
and sucked in any surrounding light.

I am the nearest to the event horizon. I shine a light from
my window as a warning – 'do not pass go.' The Government
wanted me to hand over my house to an authorized keeper. I
said 'no'. There was no way I was going to let the blackhole
suck away my history, while I was cosy in a hotel, sipping
champagne. I was born mid-heat wave in the front bedroom,
my parents were buried in a nearby field and I had never
ventured further than the county borders. They gave me a
radiation suit and left me an emergency number if I changed
my mind. The rest of the population were in the future. I was
stuck in the past.

Last night, I was woken up by the sound of the hissing
taps. I knew the plumbing had issues – my Mother used to hit
the pipes with a hammer in the winter. I was ready with my
bucket to catch any rogue drips. I opened the door and
watched the bath being pulled into the event horizon. The roll
-top swirled around as if it was being sucked down a drainage
hole. I shut the door, grabbed my duvet and slept on the sofa.

My dreams are full of the people I could not save. Many people have wandered into the blackhole. They had no hope left. One man said the blackhole had already sucked out his heart.

The blackhole moves silently, pulling at the seams of the house. When I went for an inspection this morning, I found the back bedroom was missing too. In a past life it was the honeymoon suite. It was the only room I still maintained, hoping I would one day get to snuggle between the silk sheets with a ring on my finger. The blackhole had captured by photo albums and even had my birth certificate. I no longer exist.

Chemoids

Brian George

St. David's Day. No daffodils on me today, though. Three hours of infusions, not as bad as some poor bastards who have to spend the whole day in the hospital. Then I get fitted up with my pump for the second drug, tucked into a little bumbag.

I call in the canteen for a cup of tea. Meet up with a few of the others who always have their appointments the same time as me. We call ourselves the chemoids. We have a natter, compare notes and try to laugh a bit.

There's one woman there I haven't seen before. Headscarf, grey complexion, a reminder of things I don't want to think about too much. She tries out a little smile when the rest of us laugh a bit too loud.

A gang of nurses come in for their lunch. Sound like they'd be fun to party with. They get their pies and chips, their veggie lasagnes and go to sit in the staff section. Kept separate from us chemoids. After about ten minutes we hear them start singing *Mae hen wlad fy nhadau*. Nice, upbeat tempo, not the dirge it's often turned into.

And we sing along, all the chemoids, voices a bit wavery, one or two not sure of the words after the first line, but we hold our own. The woman in the headscarf has a lovely soprano, gives the final line a real caning, an octave above all the rest. Her eyes are shining when we've finished.

Missing

Trevor Byrne

Clare Curran was on the bus when she saw her son's face on a poster:

MISSING. Sean Curran, 16 years old, last seen outside Copperface Jack's, Dublin, September 14th, 2010.

Clare had moved to Manchester soon after Sean's body was found, and this was the first time she'd been back to Dublin.

As soon as saw the poster she stood up and pressed the bell. The bus had started to climb Lower Bridge Street and she'd have to walk back.

She stepped off the bus into a part of the city she didn't know, and walked down the hill.

The poster was on a lamppost outside a pub, The Brazen Head. Behind the gates, people were in the beer garden, drinking and smoking and laughing.

A month before they left for Manchester, her husband and her daughter, Sinead, had taken the posters down, as many as they could find. Clare was angry they hadn't told her: all along, they'd kept her from her son's disappearance, as though they thought she was stupid, that they could do a better job.

Sean was missing for two days when the Guard suggested the posters. They'd need a description, including any distinguishing features, like tattoos, birthmarks or scars.

—He's none of those, said Clare.

Sinead, who was seventeen then, was sitting beside her. Clare wanted to say that Sean had his father's eyes, that he was good looking and had a gorgeous smile, but when she imagined saying this, she felt her face redden.

Sinead took over. She said that Sean had short dark hair, brushed away from his forehead, like Cristiano Ronaldo's, and a pale complexion, and cornflower blue eyes. She said it clearly and calmly.

—The photograph'll be crucial, said the Guard.

—I'll get one, said Clare. She had one in mind, from the album under the television.

—Here's a nice one, said Clare.

—That's no use, Ma, said Sinead.

—But he's lovely in that.

—It doesn't look like him, said Sinead. —That's like what you'd put on Facebook for your profile picture.

Clare wouldn't tell Sinead or her husband about this one last poster outside The Brazen Head. She'd take it down properly, and fold it nicely. She'd bring him home.

But the poster was too high, so she asked a bargirl for a chair from the beer garden to stand on. The bargirl helped by sitting on the chair while Clare stepped up, holding the lamppost.

—Is that your youngfella? said the bargirl.

The poster was fastened to the lamppost with cable ties.

—Have you a scissors? said Clare.

The bargirl went into the pub and Clare sat on the chair beneath the poster. She didn't mind waiting. It was a warm day and she had time to do this. She wanted to do this.

The bargirl stepped out of the pub and held up the scissors and smiled. She was beautiful, a girl of sixteen, maybe. Clare waved, and the bargirl moved through the laughing people towards her.

Quinquireme

Sally Zigmond

The wind whips a skipping rope of hair across my face. *Salt, mustard, vinegar, pepper. Bubble gum, bubble gum. What do you wish?* The vehicles roar down the hill like the wolf on the fold, their cohorts gleaming in purple and gold...until the lights change and I smell salt and seaweed from the sea although the city is miles away from the ocean.

'Quinquireme?' my head of department spat. 'Old-fashioned elitism. You can't expect kids to relate to that.' I shrug. Feel the words, roll them round until the edges are smooth, *Qinquireme of Ninevah. Topazes and cinnamon and gold moidores.*

Put out to grass. I swing my bag of books up the hill to where the old oak shades the bus, and off we go.

The bus swings past the Polly Garter terraces, gardens that grow washing and babies. When Mark was three I soothed him with words. *It is spring, moonless night, in the small town, silent and bible-black...* and off he'd sail into sleep.

He works in wood. Broad as an oak, sinews like saplings, soft as sawdust and poetry. *Sandalwood, cedarwood and sweet white wine.* Mark drinks Real Ale, dark and malty, rich as amber.

I took my classes to that oak before half of it split away. Robin Hood slept in this oak, I told them. See! There's Merlin curled in the silver birch. Listen! Listen to its leaves. You don't have to understand poetry to hear the rhythm of words and wood.

The bus sails on, stately Spanish galleon rising on the crest of the by-pass. The wind picks up, tossing the seagulls over the roof-tops like torn scraps of silver foil—and oh!

My bag falls onto the floor. I straighten up. The world has splintered into blocks of wood. Children's bricks of solid images scattered across the floor. *Sandalwood, cedarwood, sweet white wine.* Outside, a stiff man, scarf horizontal in the silent wind, freezes on one end of a lead attached to a wooden dog. That woman, her mouth, an open letter-box of laughter, is at the door, her arm a branch scratching the bell. The frayed man with a carved ponytail on the seat in front, dandruff like sawdust on his collar, stares, his face a chiselled gargoyle.

I lift my arm, my bag solid as my mother's mahogany sideboard. The bus is now empty of all but the driver, a cigarette in his mouth, the smoke a thumbed smudge.

More people. Wooden people. Painted clothes, uniforms. Tinker, tailor, soldier, sailor, rich man, policeman, paramedic, nurse…

I am in a bed. Mark is here. I feel the softness of cloth, the whisper of a heart, the tang of new wood, spicy as ginger. The warmth of a son. *Topazes and cinnamon and gold moidores.*

Don't speak Mum. But I do. *Ivory and apes and peacocks.*

He leans into my mouth. Picks up the words: *Firewood, iron-ware and cheap tin trays.*

Quick

Ali Smith

time gentlemen please.
Once upon a

Micro-Fiction Competition Winners:

The Worst Head in the World
Angela Readman

Liam gave me his mother's head. I guess he was sick of carrying it around.

'It's just for a while,' he said, placing the jar on the drawers. In the dark, lips made budgie-like kissing sounds. We had a reason to screw loud.

Come morning, the head tutted, 'I WANT a doily.'

It frowned if I wasted chicken bones, or didn't ask Liam if he'd washed his hands.

When he went, Liam left the head behind. It wavers in the water, tells me I'm not good enough, nods when I iron seams in jeans.

Black Hole
Dan Carpenter

There is a black hole above her house.

This swirling cosmic nothingness, ever expanding, tendrils reaching out across the sky. She does not know how it got there. She knows it's taking her things. She does not remember last Saturday. When she tries to explain it she can't. She wants to say, "There's a black hole above my house and it's stealing every memory I have ever treasured," but it is not the kind of sentence people understand.

The black hole expands, time collapses in on itself.

She discovers her twelve year old self in her attic.

Meredith

Amy Mackelden

On Grey's Anatomy, everyone's slept with everybody, and although real life is complicated, I'm sure it's not that complicated, or if it is then everyone's fucking without me, doing it secretly, when I'm at Pilates, or sleeping between ten and eight.

New Build

Clare O'Brien

There is no door to close. Just space, scaffolded, bathed in mud and builder's grit. The air rolls in, clouds of steam boiling from impervious stone, steel rods singing down into the sea.

I can already smell the tang of a fire burning at our bare hearth as the rain sweeps through the rafters. Our boys climb ladders lashed to girders, laugh at the water which sticks their shirts to their backs.

Around our house's heart the rooms are growing shells. Inside these plotted squares we'll live our story. The windows wait outside, roped against the wind.

Relieving Mafeking
Alun Williams

The 06:17 from Nuneaton stops for three minutes outside Wembley on its approach to Euston. For one hundred and eighty seconds, Mafeking Jones sits open mouthed in his usual seat, staring at a naked woman, framed like a fallen Madonna at her open bedroom window.

No one else notices, no one else sees, perhaps because they are insularly wrapped up in newsprint tales of economic gloom and sporting deeds that have now passed to memory.

Mafeking is an accountant, a man of spreadsheets and numbers but for those three Wembley solitary minutes he's Michaelangelo in a Florentine dream.

New Shoes
Jenny Adamthwaite

Dad wanted trainers.

"I'd like to know I could run away," he said.

When the hospital bed lay empty, it gave us a moment's hope.

Alterations

Tim Stevenson

After the accident she came home rebuilt.

At breakfast, the platinum beneath her skin glows, pulsing with electricity, curiously alive.

I take some toast, spread butter. I see that there are no eggs in the pan.

She smiles, a mechanical lighthouse across the blue ocean of tablecloth. Her head turns smoothly towards the window, her warmth coming only from the sun.

I open my newspaper setting the pages full sail, seeking guidance in the new star of her unreadable face, in the night of her eyes.

Tonight I know I will not dream of her, only of the sea.

Sad Lover

Jason Bagshaw

Beth and Alana had reservations at the restaurant in town. On the phone Beth said, 'I'll meet you at seven,' and Alana faked excitement and said, 'Can't wait.' Half past seven and the two of them were seated, ordering their drinks, listening to the piano of a popular composer coming through the speakers. 'It's Bach,' said Beth. 'I know,' Alana replied, but she knew it was Mozart and she wanted to break things off with her. 'I'm going to tell George everything,' said Beth and Alana cried inside. 'Good,' Alana said and hummed along to Mozart. To Bach.

First Person

Martha Williams

You lie within me, cupped and curled. You're in me, I'm in you; we're each other's inside out.

They count your fingers, toes, chromosomes... twice. My head spins.

Are you upside down?

They turn off the monitor. They speak in needles, numbers, and odds. I strum my fingers to your kicks.

They say, "If you... we have pills... the products of conception would..." They don't smile. My belly tightens.

Can you feel me? I'm your first person.

I say, "The products of conception, call them 'Emma'."

You lie still...

When you wake, you can call me 'Mum'.

She'll Leave You For A Man

Kirsty Logan

You've always known it: that gleam, that glint, that licking of lips that means she is thinking about them. Men.

She thinks about them while smelling night jasmine, while rolling out pastry, while signing the bill for the waiter.

And so she will go. She will forget the shape of your hands.

But she will tire of her stubble-rashed chin, of long silences and calloused thumbs, of nothing to pillow her head.

So wait. Just wait.

Authors

We don't have enough room in a volume such as this to list a full biography for all of our authors, and anyway, why should we when they have all already done the job for us on their blogs and websites?

So, below, please find a list of the places on the World-Wide Web where you can follow up the authors from this anthology. Please read their other work, buy their books, and generally support them. That way they can continue to bring you wonderful stories like the ones you've just read.

Jenny Adamthwaite	jadamthwaite.co.uk
Jenn Ashworth	jennashworth.co.uk
Jason Bagshaw	j.bagshaw@hotmail.co.uk
Jay Barnett	theaftermathofmygreatidea.blogspot.co.uk
Natalie Bowers	nataliebowers.org
Andy Broadey	www.bankley.org.uk/Artist-Andy-Broadey
Trevor Byrne	trevorbyrne.ie
Jen Campbell	jen-campbell.blogspot.com
Dan Carpenter	winterhillmcr.wordpress.com
Sarah-Clare Conlon	wordsandfixtures.blogspot.co.uk
L.A. Craig	@LAC00000 (Twitter)
Sara Crowley	asalted.blogspot.co.uk
Brindley Hallam Dennis	Bhdandme.wordpress.com
Carrie Etter	carrieetter.blogspot.co.uk
David Gaffney	davidgaffney.org
Nick Garrard	@nevervane (Twitter)
Vanessa Gebbie	vanessagebbie.com
Brian George	leafofbrian.blogspot.co.uk
David Gilbert	templarpoetry.com/products/liberian-pygmy-hippopotamus-by-david-gilbert
Susan F. Giles	sfgiles.wordpress.com
Eli Goldstone	pauvrelapinou.tumblr.com
Nathan Good	nathan-good.blogspot.com
Kylie Grant	bedsheetsandbiscuitcrumbs.blogspot.co.uk

Kevlin Henney	asemantic.net
Tania Hershman	taniahershman.com
Sarah Hilary	sarah-crawl-space.blogspot.co.uk
SJI Holliday	sjiholliday.com
Bob Jacobs	bobjacobs.co.uk/blog
Benjamin Judge	benjaminjudge.com
Calum Kerr	calumkerr.co.uk
Emma J. Lannie	garglingwithvimto.blogspot.co.uk
Kirsty Logan	kirstylogan.com
Amy Mackelden	july2061.com
Rupan Malakin	rupanmalakin.com
Nigel McLoughlin	nigelmcloughlin.co.uk
Erinna Mettler	erinnamettler.com
David R. Morgan	likethispress.co.uk/ publications/davidrmorgan
Nicholas Murray	www.AnnexeMagazine.com
Clare O'Brien	clarefromscotland.blogspot.co.uk
Valerie O'Riordan	valerieoriordan.com
Sal Page	sal-cobbledtogether.blogspot.co.uk
Jessica Patient	writerslittlehelper.blogspot.com
Jonathan Pinnock	jonathanpinnock.com
Dan Powell	danpowellfiction.com
Ian Rankin	ianrankin.net
Angela Readman	www.saltpublishing.com/writers/ profile.php?recordID=210731
Mark Sheerin	critcismism.com
Rin Simpson	@rinsimpson (Twitter)
Ali Smith	iterature.britishcouncil.org/ali-smith
Tim Stevenson	guideentries.blogspot.co.uk
Simon Thirsk	simonthirsk.com
Alex Thornber	alexthornber.wordpress.com
Sue Walker-Stokes	facebook.com/sue1994
Alison Wells	alisonwells.wordpress.com
Laura Wilkinson	laura-wilkinson.co.uk
Alun Williams	nationalflashfictionday.co.uk/ alunwilliams.html
Martha Williams	marthawilliams.org
Eunice Yeates	nationalflashfictionday.co.uk/ euniceyeates.html
Sally Zigmond	theelephantinthewritingroom .blogspot.co.uk

Acknowledgements

The editors would like to thank the following: Arts Council England, who have supported National Flash-Fiction Day 2012 and made this book a reality; CompletelyNovel.com for their assistance in making it a real and beautiful object; Andy Broadey for an amazing cover design; Dan Peacock for an awful lot of behind the scenes work dealing with submissions and keeping the editors sane; Vic Errington, Frances Everitt, Lorraine Mace, Nuala Ní Chonchúir, Nik Perring and Matt Shoard for saying such nice things at such short notice; all of the authors who submitted stories—successful or not—it was a pleasure to read your work; and all of our commissioned writers for bringing their words to us on time and making them such beautiful ones.

Thanks are also due to Valerie, Holly Howitt, Sarah Hilary, Sara Crowley and Nici West for doing such a good job of judging our micro-fiction competition.

And an extra thank you to absolutely everyone involved in National Flash-Fiction Day 2012 for making an idle dream come true.

Calum would like to thank Kath and Milo for putting up with him during long days putting the book together; and everyone else including in the project for helping to make it just so darn good. And, of course, special thanks to Mum and Dad, without whom...

Valerie would like to thank Seren, her most micro of fictions, who's growing more factual and macro by the day.

National Flash-Fiction DAY

16th May 2012

This anthology was created in partnership with the first ever National Flash-Fiction Day, held on 16th May 2012 to celebrate the wonder of flash-fiction.

Writers reading, readers writing, competitions, anthologies and more, National Flash-Fiction Day brings you all kinds of wonderful flash-fiction joys.

And you can be involved too!

For more information and to find out how you can become part of National Flash-Fiction Day, visit

www.nationalflashfictionday.co.uk

or find us on Facebook at

facebook.com/nationalflashfictionday

or on Twitter at

@nationalflashfd